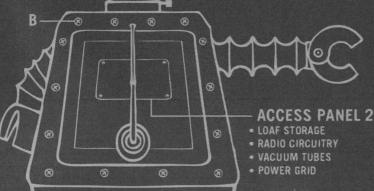

ACCESS PANEL 1
- HEATING ELEMENTS
- BINOCULAR CAMERA
- MOTIVATIONAL CONDUIT
(ETIQUETTE AND ZEAL CONTROL)

ACCESS PANEL 2
- LOAF STORAGE
- RADIO CIRCUITRY
- VACUUM TUBES
- POWER GRID

(3) **REAR VIEW**

CRUMB
EXPULSION
PANEL

(4) **BOTTOM VIEW**
(LIMBS REMOVED)

(B) **LEG SECTION**
SHOCK ABSORPTION DETAIL
NOT TO SCALE

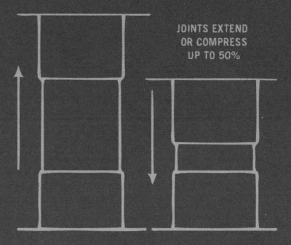

JOINTS EXTEND
OR COMPRESS
UP TO 50%

GENERAL NOTES

1. THIS MODEL (3674A) IS INTENDED FOR INDOOR USE ONLY. FOR REFITTING OF LEG SECTIONS WITH TRACTOR TREAD, REFER TO PLAN A004.

2. THIS MODEL IS NOT SUITABLE FOR IMMERSION. FOR UNDERWATER TOASTING APPARATUSES, REFER TO PLAN A007.

3. THIS MODEL MAY BE FITTED WITH A WAFFLE IRON HEAD. SEE PLAN A009.

4. ARMS ARE DESIGNED FOR UP TO 190 DEGREES OF LATERAL ARTICULATION. FURTHER ARTICULATION MAY RESULT IN DISLOCATION. LUBRICATE ARM JOINTS WITH MACHINE OIL OR UNSALTED BUTTER.

5. CONTRACTOR IS ADVISED NOT TO CONVERSE WITH ANY COMPLETED MODEL. THIS ASSOCIATION MAY RESULT IN EMOTIONAL ATTACHMENT AND CONSEQUENT RELUCTANCE OF CONTRACTOR TO RELEASE MODEL/S FOR DISTRIBUTION.

6. CONTRACTOR IS REQUIRED TO TEST EACH MODEL'S RADIO RECEIVER FOR EFFICACY. HOWEVER, THE RADIO SHOULD NOT BE LEFT ON FOR ANY DURATION, AS DANCING MAY RESULT—A SAFETY HAZARD IN MOST FACTORY SETTINGS.

7. CONTRACTOR IS REQUIRED TO TEST EACH MODEL'S HEATING ELEMENTS, BUT IS ADVISED AGAINST PREPARING TOAST FOR CONSUMPTION. THIS MAY PROMOTE EXCESSIVE SNACKING AND CRUMB ACCUMULATION.

8. LOAF STORAGE IS TO BE HEAT SANITIZED AFTER MODEL CONSTRUCTION, BUT NOT FILLED. BREAD WILL BE SUPPLIED BY RETAILER.

ROBOCO INC.
ROCHESTER, NEW YORK

DRAWN BY
Winston Foobcam

ISSUED FOR:
August 22, 1938

DRAWING No.
A003

clink

Manufactured by **KELLY DiPUCCHIO**
and **MATTHEW MYERS**

BALZER+BRAY
An Imprint of *HarperCollins*Publishers

Balzer + Bray is an imprint of HarperCollins Publishers.

Clink

Library of Congress Cataloging-in-Publication Data
DiPucchio, Kelly S.
    Clink / manufactured by Kelly DiPucchio and Matthew Myers. — 1st ed.
        p. cm.
    Summary: While newer, fancier robots are quickly purchased, Clink, an
old-fashioned robot who can only make toast and music, gathers dust and feels
downhearted until a young boy enters the shop looking for something special.
        ISBN 978-0-06-192928-1 (trade bdg.)
        ISBN 978-0-06-192929-8 (lib. bdg.)
        [1. Robots—Fiction. 2. Self-esteem—Fiction.] I. Myers, Matthew, date, ill.
II. Title.
PZ7.D6219Cli 2011   2009030834
[E]—dc22   CIP
                                                                                  AC

11 12 13 14 15   SCP   10 9 8 7 6 5 4 3 2 1
❖
First Edition

For Pat and John DiPucchio,
whose home is always filled with
lots of love and cookies.
—K.D.

Thanks, Dad, for teaching me
how to draw. Thanks, Mom, for
teaching me what to draw.
—M.M.

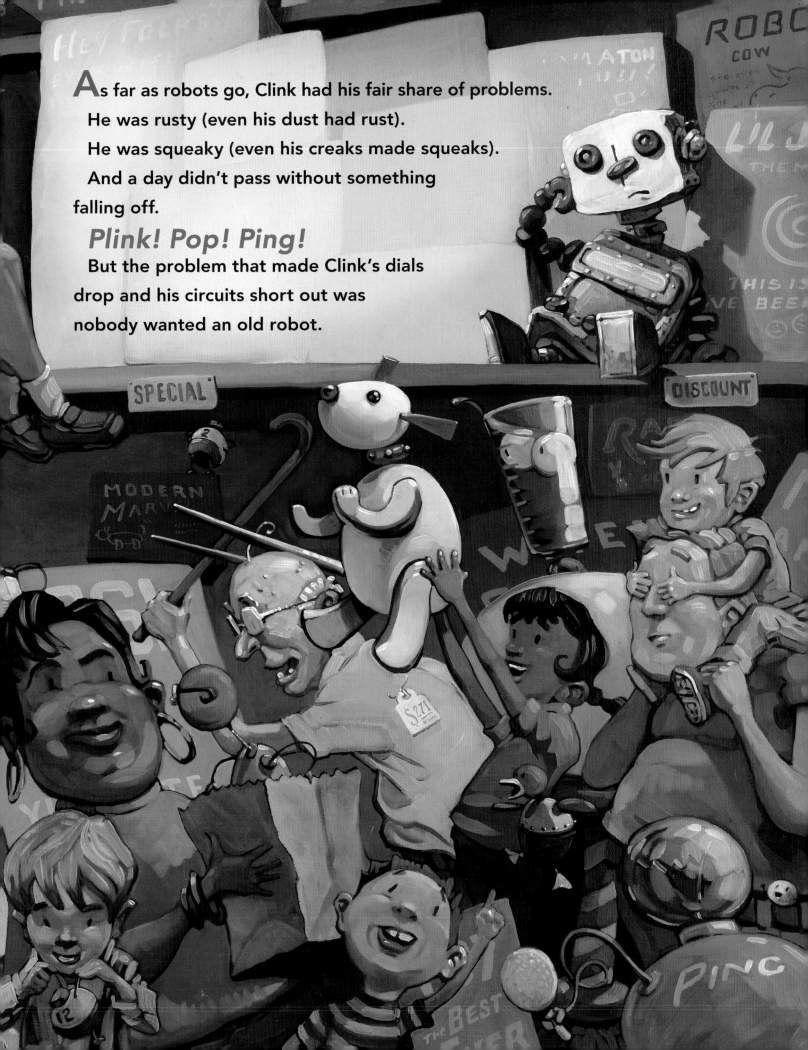

As far as robots go, Clink had his fair share of problems.

He was rusty (even his dust had rust).

He was squeaky (even his creaks made squeaks).

And a day didn't pass without something falling off.

Plink! Pop! Ping!

But the problem that made Clink's dials drop and his circuits short out was nobody wanted an old robot.

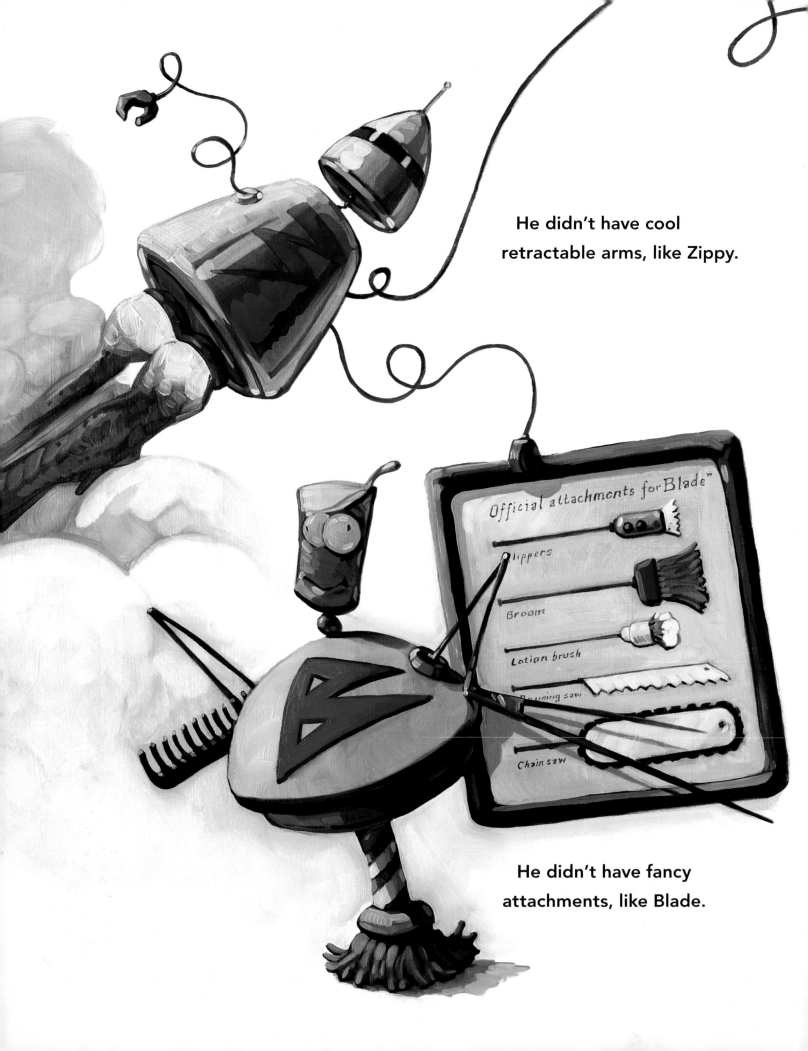

He didn't have cool retractable arms, like Zippy.

He didn't have fancy attachments, like Blade.

And he didn't know the first thing about doing homework and baking chocolate chip cookies, like Penny.

The world, it seemed, was no longer interested in a robot who had been programmed to play music and make toast.

When people came into the store, they marveled at Zippy's ability to pick up dirty laundry and play baseball at the same time. When Clink tried to do the same, everybody just laughed.

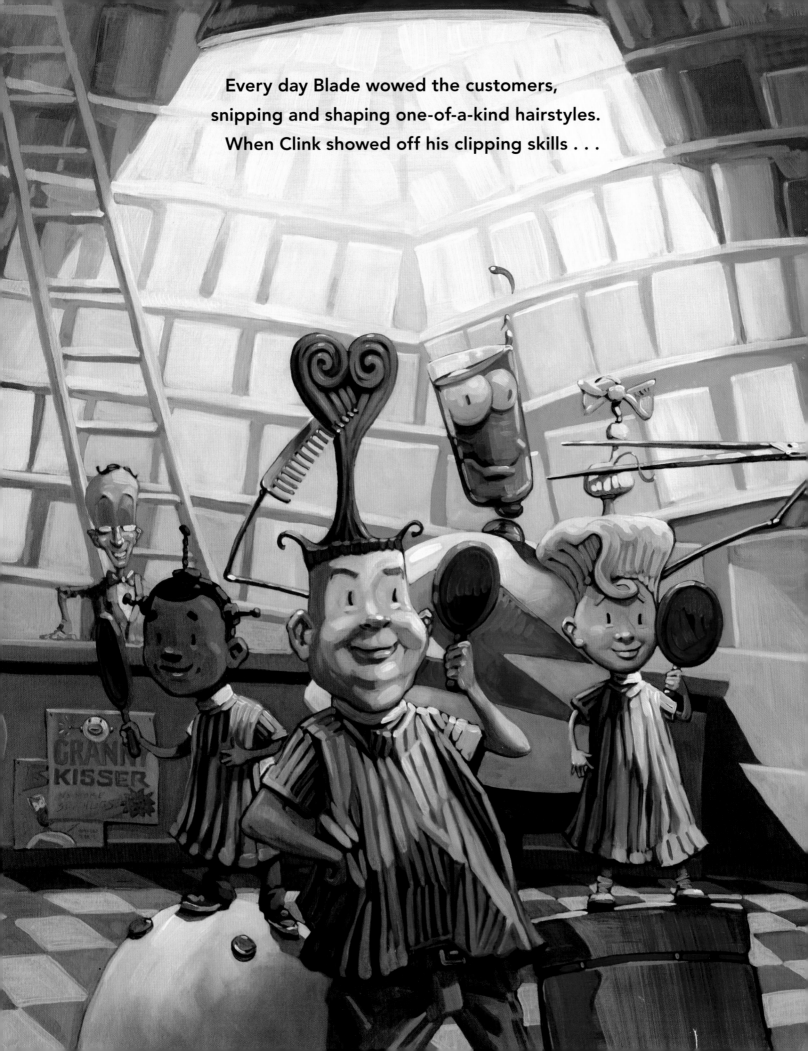

Every day Blade wowed the customers,
snipping and shaping one-of-a-kind hairstyles.
When Clink showed off his clipping skills . . .

the results were usually disastrous.

And when children lined up around the store to sample one of Penny's warm chocolate chip cookies, nobody, not even the store mice, seemed interested in Clink's dry toast.

At night, when the store was closed for the evening,
the other robots tried their best to keep Clink's spirits up.
Penny gave him cookies.
Blade gave him a makeover.
And Zippy gave him a pair of underpants. (He meant well.)

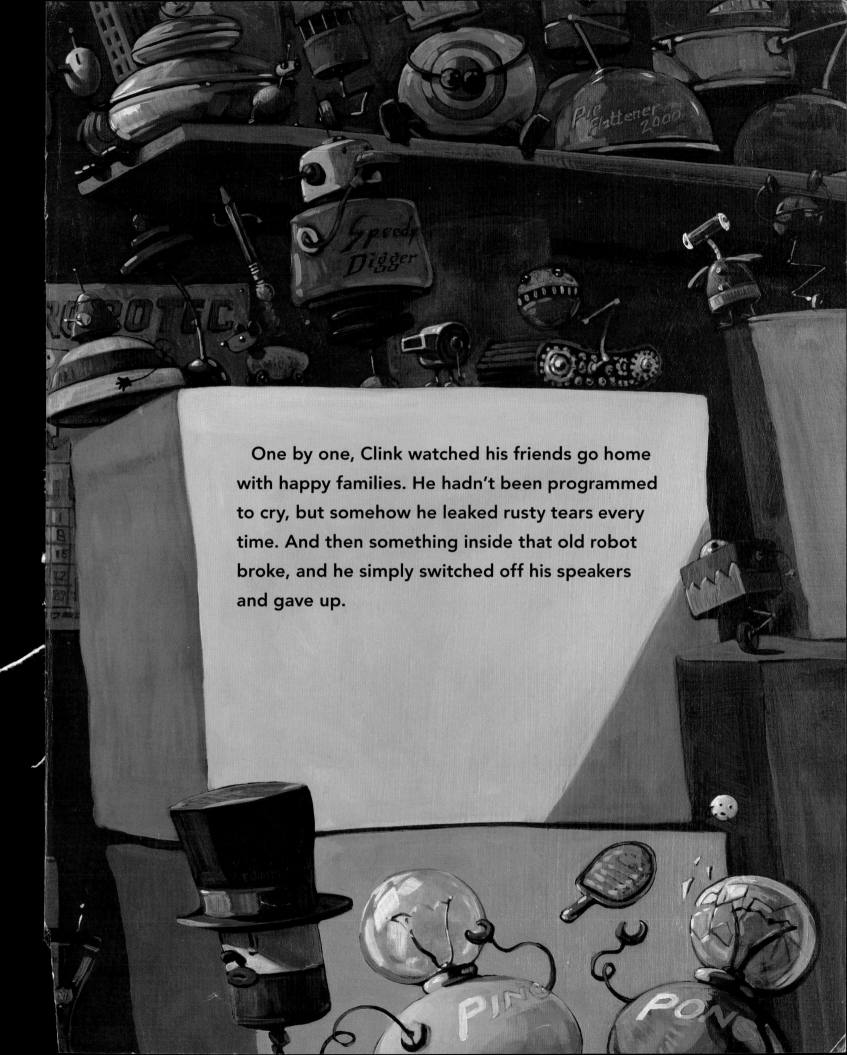

One by one, Clink watched his friends go home with happy families. He hadn't been programmed to cry, but somehow he leaked rusty tears every time. And then something inside that old robot broke, and he simply switched off his speakers and gave up.

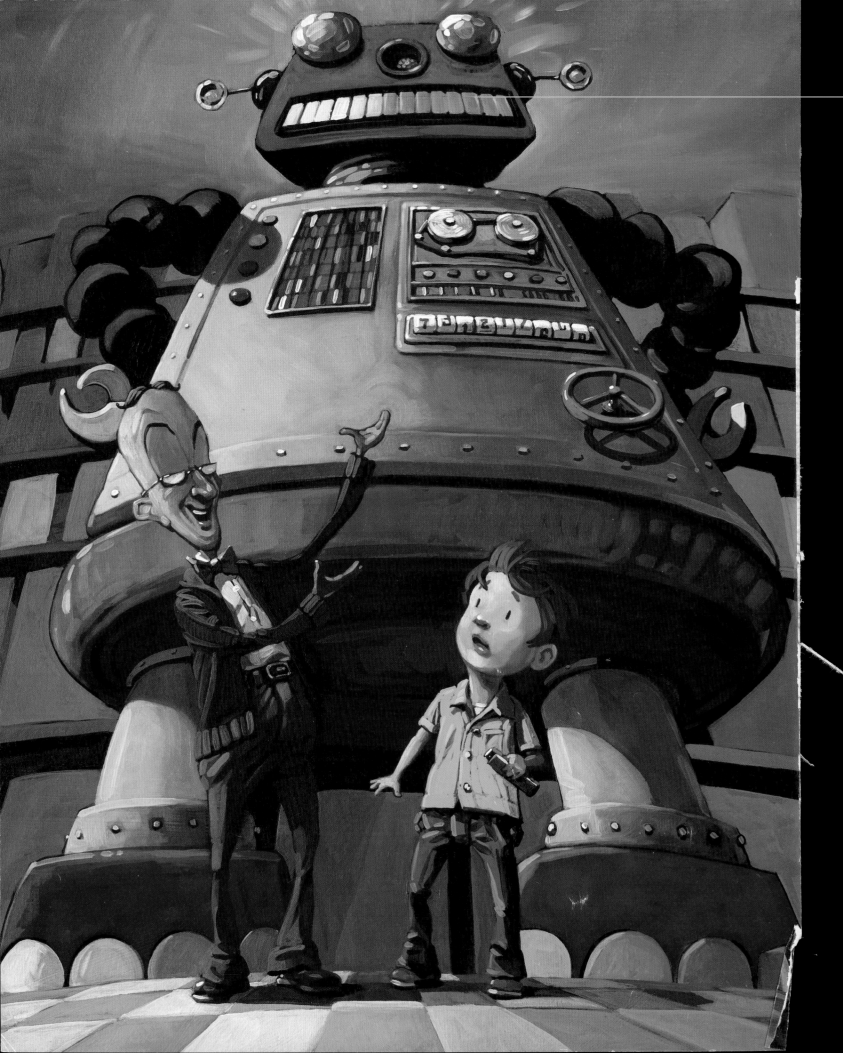

Many weeks later a young boy came into the store. It was the same boy who stopped by every week to look around but never bought a thing. Nevertheless, the proud shopkeeper always welcomed an opportunity to show off his brightest and best new robots.

"Behold the Amazing Colossal Bot!"

"Too big," said the boy.

"Twinky?"

"Too pinky."

"Bongo?"

"TOO BOUNCY!"

Nothing the shopkeeper showed him was just right. The boy was about to leave when Clink heard the happy hum of music.

Suddenly the squeaky gears in his head began to turn again, and he got an idea.

Clink stood up tall, brushed off the dust and cobwebs . . .

YES, WE HAVE GORT VII

AS SEEN ON TV

MILLIBOT

and belted out a head-boppin', toast-poppin',
showstoppin' tune.

The song was old-fashioned and crackled with static,
but there was pure joy in every note.

The boy turned around.

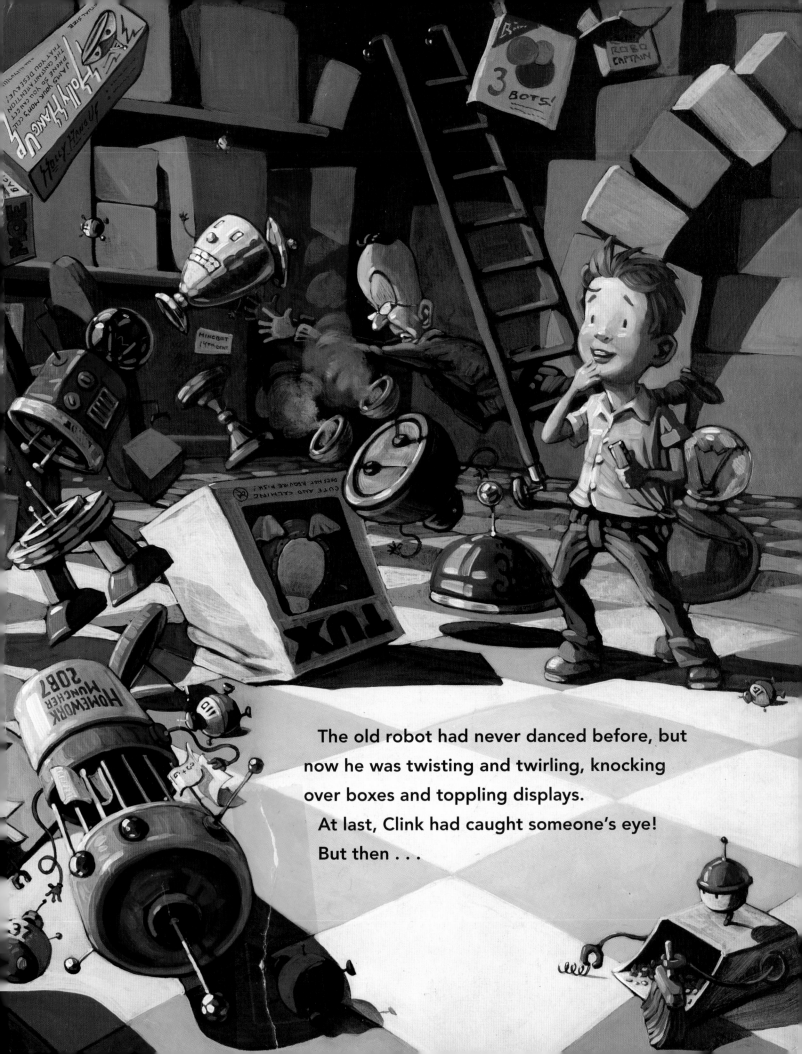

The old robot had never danced before, but
now he was twisting and twirling, knocking
over boxes and toppling displays.
At last, Clink had caught someone's eye!
But then . . .

Plink! Pop! Ping!

. . . a rusty spring hit the young customer
square in the forehead.
The music stopped.

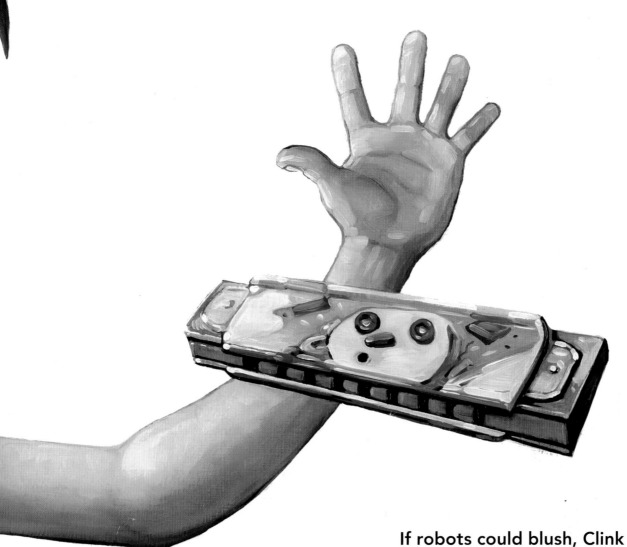

If robots could blush, Clink
would have turned a hot shade
of fire engine red.

"Oh! So sorry!" cried the shopkeeper. "I've never seen him act like this before!"

"Wait!" said the boy. "May I see him first?"

"This troublemaker?"

The shopkeeper handed Clink to the boy.

"He's very old, and he's missing parts."

The boy's eyes lit up.
"He's perfect!"

"I'm perfect?" thought Clink. It had been a very long time since anybody had thought he was perfect.

Clink smiled.

Plink! Pop!

The boy ducked. "I'll take him!" he said.

And so, as far as robots go, Clink had his fair share of good luck, too. He went home with his new friend, Milton, who, as it turns out, likes burned toast, is great at fixing things, and . . .

loves to dance.

FOR REVIEW AND COORDINATION

1/8 SCALE

LEGEND
R............RIVET
B............BOLT
V............VENT
VT...........VACUUM TUBE

POWER GRID LAYOUT

VT
(X16)

30-400 PSI GRIP CAPABILITY

R

(A)

CLAW ARTICULATION DETAIL

NOT TO SCALE

(1) **SIDE VIEW**

R

COMPRESSION NECK JOINT

32" NORMAL
FUNCTIONING HEIGHT

38" FULLY EXTENDED

R

B

V

8" MAX.

5"-7"

BREAD SLICE PARAMETERS
(FOR OTHER BREADSTUFF
SPECIFICATIONS
REFER TO PLAN A0013B)

ANTENNA
COLLAPSIBLE TO 6" & EXTENDABLE TO 16"

RADIO DIAL
TUNING RATIO:
3 KNOB ROTATIONS PER FREQUENCY

6 5 7 8 9 10 12
5 60 65 70 80 90 100 120

(2) **FRONT VIEW**

ARMS EXTEND
FROM 6" TO 18"

R

B

TUNER

AM/FM SELECTION

VOLUME CONTROL

HAM RADIO

COMPRESSION LEG JOINTS
(SEE DETAIL B)

V

CONSULTING ENGINEERS

RALPH JONES P.C.
194 20TH STREET
GREAT NECK, TENNESSEE
KLONDIKE 4-9230

GIANFRANCO GILBERTO
1841 GABINETTO STREET
MUCKLEBROOK, MICHIGAN
IDLEWOOD 6-4000

C L I N K
DOMESTIC AUTOMATON

MODEL No. 3674A
PATENT No. 016943